Advance Praise for *Norm*

"What I love about the poems in *Normal Distance* is how each uncannily assembles within the reader a scale model of Gabbert's own booming wonder—a New Mexico moon rises 'absurd on its face. // All ha ha ha.' Sleep is where 'Time comes out of time'; then, it's 'a performance for God.' It's all just so delight-full, delight in the Horatian sense of *dulce et util*, delight that pierces the reader's mind so wisdom can get in. Gabbert achieves that highest lyric aim: she restores to living a bit of its baffle."

—Kaveh Akbar, author of *Pilgrim Bell*

"Reading Elisa Gabbert's *Normal Distance* is like seeing through 'a mirror at strange angles,' where contradiction and paradox fascinate and stymie the human drive to know. I loved wandering with Gabbert through extended, long-lined meditations and drilling down with her into short intense lyrics on the eternal subjects—suffering, boredom, madness, the moon—like I'd been taken in hand by a mad hatter epistemologist, wondering why we think we know what we know. You can use *Normal Distance* for bibliomancy, opening its pages at random to find just the right words for what ails you, and what might lift your mind and spirit too. It's friendly and surprising, thinking with Gabbert: her wit is sly, her apprehension of the ordinary so strange and

true: 'We are born not remembering why we walked into the room.'" —Dana Levin, author of
Now Do You Know Where You Are

"'I feel,' says Kierkegaard's aesthete 'A,' 'as if I were a piece in a game of chess, when my opponent says of it: That piece cannot be moved!' But in this playfully despairing book, our speaker— call her the melancholy American—feels to me like she's on third base with (a) the bases loaded and (b) the distinct feeling that the batter's going to get walked. He does, she saunters, and, refreshingly free of ballyhoo, she scores. The poems in *Normal Distance* find Elisa Gabbert taking her trademark even-keeled clairvoyance and matter-of-fact sass to new extremes of quotidiana, new cul-de-sacs in the abyss. Say them and they'll eat at you all day." —Graham Foust, author of
Embarrassments

"A magnificent book of poems, unafraid to interrogate our maddening existence, vengefully honest, and pierced with a blazing conversation towards philosophy. Gabbert has a gift for exposing human longing, with poker-faced lyricism, for the fantasy it often is. Suffering pervades this book: our addiction to it, our denial of it, and the absolute inevitability of it. What Gabbert shows us is that suffering comes in many forms, and one of the most prevalent is boredom: 'The secret to immortality is boredom. If you're bored enough you'll never die,' she writes. Always there is a solidarity in the poems. We are all together in this; we are the poet. And humor—which Freud knew held as much rich unconscious content as dreams—makes these elegant, genius poems anything but boring. 'Can you not pay attention to your desires?,' she asks. She replies with all her pitch-perfect characteristic sagacity: 'I don't care. I want to change my mind.' Same."

—Bianca Stone, author of
What Is Otherwise Infinite

"Elisa Gabbert's newest book of poems, *Normal Distance*, is a must-read. It is a work of full force and cannot be forgotten long after you close its pages. Its intricate language mazes and areas of language play create a landscape of full sensations, thoughts, and pure emotion. In the book, you enter places where the starkness of our time is met with the tenderness of what it means to be a human. Places where the 'lindens' both 'bloom' and 'didn't bloom,' where 'suffering was less absurd,' places where the 'inflection of a spell' 'turns off your power,' where 'everything is a monolith,' places with 'frightening' 'empty space,' and where 'youth is a kind of genius.' These poems are places where anything can be anything and where what the poet feels intimately can still be everything. As Gabbert writes, 'We are born not remembering why we walked into the room,' and I believe her. This is a book that you will remember for a long time, after birth and death, and into the eternal space where poetry still lives."

—Dorothea Lasky, author of *Milk*

"'There's a hole in your nightmare / You could fall down,' writes Elisa Gabbert from America of the 2020s, where 'normal' has never been 'normal' and now distance is up in your face. 'Every year, when the lindens bloom, I think of the year / when the lindens didn't bloom,' begins this journey wherein distraction helps thinking and precision allows perspective, and indecision, which by now is a character trait of a large group, touches on metaphysical: 'Everything reminds me of it, but I don't know what "it" is.' But Gabbert knows answers, and isn't afraid to share them: 'We are born not remembering why we walked into the room.' She knows, too, that 'What it wants is desire. / A barrier to crossing / The chasm of the day.' The metaphysics in this book is felt, and lived, and searching. The questions are playful, the answers are wise, and the language is always precise, beautiful. *Normal Distance* is a joy to read and reread."

—Ilya Kaminsky, author of

Deaf Republic and *Dancing in Odessa*

"If you were to start Elisa Gabbert's sharp and companionable new book by reading the Notes, you'd find the tracks of

a restless thinker whose trip through the past—what has been written, thought, said, felt—is lined with the present-tense vertigo(s) of self-doubt, forgetfulness, anxiety, pain, joy. But don't start at the end: read this sequence from the start, open to its unfolding entanglement of quick revelations, 'The way you fail to see, or recognize yourself, in a mirror at strange angles.' Like its unresolvable title, *Normal Distance* vibrates between assertiveness and mystery, poking at philosophy's rules and continually returning us to questions of a less containable sort: how and what the body knows, and how and what the body of the poem might tell."   —Anna Moschovakis, author of
Eleanor, or, The Rejection of the Progress of Love

Select Praise for *The Unreality of Memory*

A *New York Times* Editors' Choice
A Colorado Book Award Finalist

"Gabbert draws masterly portraits of the precise, uncanny affects that govern our psychological relationship to calamity—from survivor's guilt to survivor's elation, to the awe and disbelief evoked by spectacles of destruction, to the way we manage anxiety over impending dangers. Even more impressive is her skill at bending crisp, clear language into shapes that illustrate the shifting logic of the disastrous, keeping the reader oriented amid continual upheaval." —Alexandra Kleeman,

The New York Times

"Gabbert moves fluidly from disaster to dislocation to political upheaval, offering a kind of literary road map to our tumultuous era . . . Her questing, restless intelligence is what holds the essays together . . . A fine collection from a poet who seems equally comfortable in prose." —*Kirkus Reviews* (starred review)

"Whatever the chosen topic, Gabbert's essays manage to be by turns poetic, philosophical, and exhaustively researched. This is a superb collection." —*Publishers Weekly*

"Gabbert's voice is calm, playfully engaging and clear—a voice for our anxious, wired times, if ever there was one . . . Each diligently researched essay seems to evolve organically and if she doomscrolls her way down a rabbit hole, you know it will lead somewhere not just pertinent, but poetic and philosophical too."

—*The Guardian*

"As a philosopher of disaster—imminent, recurring, and farflung—Gabbert knows there's no time to waste . . . This work lays bare the intractable chasm between what we fear and what we understand." —Rachel Vorona Cote, *The Nation*

"How did she so clearly see what was coming for us? One answer is that she has read and thought a lot about disaster and human perception, the themes that tie her essays together. Another is that she's good at finding angles readers might not otherwise see. Like a restless photographer, she'll stretch herself to find another and then another shot. She'll zoom way in and way out."

—*The Washington Post*

Select Praise for *The Word Pretty*

A *New York Times* Editors' Choice

"Like any good magpie, Gabbert keeps the delightful facts coming, and often leads into them the way she might at a dinner party . . . In just three or four paragraphs, she brilliantly parses something you might have felt about dozens of memoirs without ever putting it quite this way." —John Williams,
The New York Times Book Review

"An assemblage of layers, Gabbert's book acquires density and heft through its strategy of accumulation, creating a rich work of literary reflection that invites the reader to explore the works under consideration, as well as the wider world, from multiple, perpetually fresh perspectives." —Melynda Fuller,
Los Angeles Review of Books

"All the individual essays feel meaningfully connected, like the balls on the pool table. Although the pattern they form may appear to be random, the leave has been cleverly chosen, and the shot goes in."   —Michalle Gould, *Chicago Review of Books*

Normal Distance

Normal Distance

Poems

Elisa Gabbert

New York
Soft Skull

First Soft Skull edition: 2022

Library of Congress Cataloging-in-Publication Data
Names: Gabbert, Elisa, author.
Title: Normal distance : poems / Elisa Gabbert.
Description: First Soft Skull edition. | New York :
    Soft Skull, 2022.
Identifiers: LCCN 2021060628 | ISBN 9781593767334
    (paperback) | ISBN 9781593767341 (ebook)
Subjects: LCGFT: Poetry.
Classification: LCC PS3607.A227 N67 2022 |
    DDC 811/.6—dc23
LC record available at https://lccn.loc.gov/2021060628

Cover design by Nicole Caputo
Cover art by www.houseofthought.io
Book design by Wah-Ming Chang

Published by Soft Skull Press
New York, NY
www.softskull.com

Printed in the United States of America

10 9 8 7 6 5 4 3 2 1

I lived in the present, which was
that part of the future you could see.

LOUISE GLÜCK,
from "Landscape"

Contents

Normal Distance

Prelude

Every year, when the lindens bloom, I think of the year
when the lindens didn't bloom.

This year, so far, the lindens haven't bloomed.

I think of the year when the lindens didn't bloom.

An idea almost comes, or it comes in disguise—it's the
same old thought, but today it is startling.

The way you fail to see, or recognize yourself, in a mirror
at strange angles.

Thoughts almost arrive.

The way an owl swoops between two black trees, only at
dusk, the dusk of evening—

Morning, of course, has its own foreshortened, clandestine
dusk.

Dusk of morning. The light unblue.

Original thought was the mere idea, idea with no shadow.

The thought everafter is only shadow, and shadows are startling.

About Suffering

Part of suffering is the useless urge to announce you're suffering.

There is no other way to say it: I'm suffering. Just to say "I suffer" helps.

I read somewhere, "we become lyrical when we suffer."

Happiness is suffering for the right reasons.

First-order suffering is second-order happiness.

You have to suffer for beauty? Because you have to suffer.

We pride ourselves on a high quality of suffering.

Turgenev was born in 1818 in the province of Orel, and suffered during his childhood from a tyrannical mother.

In the past their suffering was less absurd.

The problem is, everything's worse. Paper or plastic?
We're all still going to die suffering.

I value being alone with my thoughts, but it's weird to
say, "This thing that makes us suffer less, we have to stop
doing it."

Isn't it kind of the point of culture to assuage our feeling
needless and alone?

How does one suffer "gladly," exactly?

At least the rich get to suffer in comfort.

It makes the life feel longer. Live to suffer another day.

One's past suffering can be a great source of comfort. A
torturous luxury. Velvet upholstery.

Suffering is happiness, after forty minutes of desolate
shuffling. The point is, life is suffering.

About suffering, no one is ever wrong.

The Idea of Beginning

My brother knows how to make a chair from the little wire cage on a bottle of champagne.

I find it hard to throw away the wire when I know there's a chair inside.

A chair my brother would have made, which would make it worth saving.

I find it hard to throw out flowers, which were dead on arrival.

Some philosophers think that your phone has a conscious "mind."

Same for anything sufficiently connected—like Pando, a tree that manifests as hundreds of trees and is "currently thought to be dying."

I haven't seen a crow in a long time—do crows have a season?

I got a book about symbols in the mail and it opened to the "crow" page—I'm not lying.

It said, *Because of its black colour, the crow is associated with the idea of beginning.*

Once, driving south through New Mexico at sunset, the sunset was endless.

I am not sure why, geographically or astronomically speaking, it just kept glowing.

I associate the idea of beginning with the idea of death: to exist at all is to enter eternity.

I associate the word *thing* with false humility—who am I to name a thing?

Who am I with this long blond hair?

Who am I when I sleep so deeply I wake up thinking of my childhood bed?

In New Mexico the moon rising over the mountain was absurd on its face.

All ha ha ha.

When It's Hot It Snows

There's a hole in your nightmare
You could fall down, a trapdoor, an old well.
Don't go there.

Say any word
With the inflection of a spell.
This turns off your power.

You have no more wishes.
You're in the just past, a figure of history.
It makes you significant.

You know how you die.
Can you smoke cigarettes?
Can you make choices.

You're a beautiful woman
In a black-and-white photo, forever,
Answering a rotary phone.

New Theories on Boredom

Once as a kid, I was so bored at my parents' office that I made a deck of cards.

My brother had a really boring snake who only moved when you dumped a bag of live crickets into its cage.

I wonder what would bore a tortoise.

How bored are dogs? Pretty bored, I think.

I'm kind of interested in people using two stars to mean "I got bored and didn't finish it."

I don't trust books that aren't a little boring.

It's almost like there should be different words for "boring because simple" and "boring because complex."

"Boring because complex" isn't actually boring, it can just be mistaken for boring, the way a hangover can be mistaken for guilt.

You can call this banality versus tedium, or "good boring" versus "bad boring." Kubrick movies are often great while also boring.

Whether something is boring or not has nothing to do with how good it is.

You could also call "boring because complex" interesting-boring (boring in an interesting way) or slow-interesting (interesting, but at a pace that sometimes resembles boredom).

All good poetry is slow-interesting.

I often wonder why having a beverage makes something boring more interesting. To put it another way, I love drinking while I'm bored.

I wonder why we don't get bored in the shower.

Michel Siffre lived alone in a cave in Texas for six months and got so bored he contemplated suicide, making it look like an accident.

I heard on the radio that lazy people have higher IQs—

because their minds are more active, they don't get bored doing nothing.

I don't think this is true.

Some people outside are having a boring conversation about dogs in general.

When it rains it's boring.

When it rains it bores holes into your body. Turns out it was acid rain!

Being so bored you actually start crying must be a really transformative experience.

To me, sex is not art. Once it's over it's boring again.

We're in the bargaining stage of civilization, and it's boring.

Civilization got bored with itself.

Pretty cool how we've evolved to find peace boring!

You can only be bored *almost* to death.

"This is boring." "No, it interrogates boringness!" "This is doggerel." "No, it interrogates talent!"

What, poets can't be bored by eclipses?

How boring not to have a crush on anyone.

Did you ever have a kiss so bad you felt like *you* were the bad kisser?

I think this is related to how boring people make me feel boring.

Did you know that you can trick people into being more interesting by being more interesting yourself?

I used to be bored around my parents, which made them boring. In my thirties I was shocked to learn I didn't know everything about them.

So if you have to spend time with boring people, try being DAZZLING.

My most common thought while lucid dreaming is *God, what a boring dream.*

I'm glad Andre Gregory knows the Andre character is a "raging narcissist" bore.

My TED Talk topic would be "*Jiro Dreams of Sushi* Is Not an Enjoyable Movie."

I would just make people watch it and stop it every now and then to say, "See? This is boring and oppressive."

A totally fascist approach to sushi.

I sometimes think *After Hours* is the worst movie that's anyone's favorite movie.

I associate it strongly with *Joe Versus the Volcano*, since I think of both as somehow "angry boring."

It takes a special kind of mediocrity to be offensive and boring at the same time.

If the language is boring, there should at least be some emotions or ideas or something.

Boring through, or thoroughly boring?

I was very boring today.

Sometimes the dystopia was boring.

At least everyone was boring at the same time about something inherently interesting.

Sometimes it feels like if I'm not fascinated, I'm bored.

Wild Animals (Normal Distance)

Watching silent films in a backyard at night, I'm distracted
by a bat fluttering overhead, its flight path so erratic.

A moth made bright in the projector light.

The day before in the park, there were so many midges in
"the middle distance" we couldn't estimate their number.

Thousands? Hundreds of thousands?

A raccoon in the vines on a telephone pole . . .

Baby bunny in the grass . . .

However cute, I like to imagine it might be rabid.

I think a little threat is necessary for happiness.

I think sometimes we want to be threatened, sometimes
we want to be the threat.

Sometimes when I'm standing what feels like a normal distance from a person, they keep seeming to edge away.

I must keep edging closer too, or the effect would stop happening, but it continues.

Like when you go into the ocean, you never come out where you went in.

I'm trying to decide if Wittgenstein was sexy. It's not obvious.

I think the answer is "yes" or "unanswerable."

I think delicate people are frightening.

But I also think fear is erotic.

Wittgenstein believed his *Tractatus* was the last work of philosophy that would ever "need" to be written—that he had answered all the important questions.

He quit philosophy for a while and became an architect . . .

He built a house for his sister she wouldn't live in . . .

Einstein believed that publishing his theory of relativity would end all thinking about time.

Now scientists believe we have a mirror universe, a "reflection" of our universe where time flows backward from the future to the past.

The "arrow of time" either points in one direction or in two directions, forward and back.

Why not in all directions, like a minute hand? Or in *all* directions, like everything?

I want to experience my past again, but as I was then, doing what I did then—nothing changed.

In what sense, then, am I not living through it, again and again?

Isn't the past always *happening*?

The Vagueness of the Moment

I saw a dead bunny in the grass, all bloody and ravaged—
First by a dog or a hawk and now covered in ants.
I stopped to look at it but did not photograph it.

There's no time for mourning; the deaths fall
Into the void of unceremony
And become one death.

It's not some monolith, they say about everything,
But everything is a monolith,
A wave that never collapses.

I play an eight-hour track of rain sounds on windows
All day on a loop. The sky is too high
And I want to feel crushed.

The vagueness of the moment
Has a crispness in memory,
Like mountains from a distance.

I'm Not Mourning (There Is Voids)

I had it again, the dream that I lose my bags in the airport and miss my flight to Paris.

Every time, it's devastating.

I've never been to Paris, in real life or in a dream.

Awake, I sometimes feel that it's too late (in history) to go to Paris.

Paris syndrome is a state of "extreme shock" experienced by travelers forced to reconcile Paris-in-reality with their expectations—it can cause acute anxiety, despair, hallucinations, delusions, and "depersonalization," the impression of observing yourself from the outside.

The sense that your self has left your body—you have *depersoned*.

Unlike Stendhal syndrome, a condition that occurs when one is overcome by the beauty and profundity of great art,

Paris syndrome is the result of "immense disappointment" in the face of the banality of Paris.

Even in Kyoto, I long for Kyoto.

In the mourning journal he wrote in the months following his mother's death in 1977, Roland Barthes quotes Donald Winnicott: "The catastrophe you *fear* will happen has *already* happened."

Less than three years after his mother, Barthes died from injuries sustained when he was hit by a laundry van while walking through the streets of Paris.

Pierre Curie was also killed in the streets of Paris, in 1906. He fell in the rain, and a horse-drawn cart wheeled over his head.

He was already weakened by massive exposure to radiation.

From Marie Curie's mourning journal: "My Pierre, the life is atrocious without you, it is an anguish without name."

There is almost something romantic about dying from "complications."

Romanticism makes of all death a romance.

According to legend, in 1794, grave robbers stole Shakespeare's skull.

In 2016, an archaeologist used radar to confirm that his skull is not in his tomb: "What we found is that half of his grave is undisturbed. And then the head end, so where his skull would have been, there is voids."

Georges Perec's novel *A Void* (the English title of *La Disparition*—the disappearance) does not contain the letter *e*.

To adhere to the constraint, it might also have been translated *A Vanishing*.

Perec, born Peretz, an orphan, died outside Paris, from lung cancer, in 1982.

Every death is a fact.

Barthes writes: "Don't say *Mourning* . . . I'm not *mourning*. I'm suffering."

That to Philosophize Is to Learn to Die

There was a metal band that was just called Death.

I used to think I wasn't afraid of death, but actually what I wasn't afraid of was being dead.

You can't attend your own funeral, but you have to attend your own death.

You are going to die of something.

I hope I die of boredom in my sleep.

Do you ever remember being so excited about the future you were afraid you might die before it happened?

I mean, who cares, of course, democracy is dead.

Death wish, free will, cause and effect, happiness as misery.

I wonder if the wealthy dinosaurs were the last to die.

Hemingway titled a book *Death in the Afternoon*, which is the best possible name for a cocktail, then invented a cocktail named after it. I am extremely jealous of this whole move.

I don't *actually* want to die laughing.

"Only one image of Virginia Eliza Clemm Poe has been authenticated: a watercolor portrait painted several hours after her death."

There was 100% a culture of dead bodies are cool.

Is a beautiful woman still beautiful even if all men everywhere are dead?

Vanity ends with death.

Who wants to be present in the moment? I want to die when an asteroid hits my cryogenic chamber.

Naps, but for death.

You can't actually sleep when you're dead.

The secret to immortality is boredom. If you're bored enough you'll never die.

Die with dignity like Benjamin Guggenheim.

Death by attrition. War of natural causes.

Death has an anchoring, as in dragging-down, effect, so, don't die.

"Sex" and "death" kind of rhyme.

You can sleep in your deathbed.

Sappho: "To die is evil. The gods think so, Else they would die."

Cry now, die later. Move to Europe, smoke and die cool.

I want to die someday.

I don't want to die laughing.

Madness

It's not my hands that are shaking—it's my mind.
Cut off my head!
That's where the pain lies.

Mishima believed sincerity was found in the entrails.
This must be a mistranslation.
I think he meant reality.

Hope is the dark part of morning,
The trees and not the sky behind.
A glimmer without a color.

Most people want justice
But in absence of justice
They will take vengeance.

As if dying was peak existence.
We called it sweet
In the cherry season of history.

You Don't Get to Decide How to Feel About Not Having Free Will

I heard more babies are born when there's a full moon and "no one knows why."

A few days later I heard it's a myth.

I heard there are land tides—and this is true—the moon pulls the *land* up.

Simone de Beauvoir said, *I cannot appropriate the snow field where I slide.*

The fundamental ambiguity: How am I unlike the field, when I am like the field, to the field?

(Not like anything at all.)

I wonder if mothers are tidal—if there are tides in the womb.

Grave and *gravity* don't share the same root.

Yesterday, I was gazing out the window and saw a squirrel try to jump from the roof of a house to a tree branch and miss.

For a second it scrambled for purchase in midair—it recognized its own death.

It looked so human, like a stuntman.

Was there time for fear, in squirrel time?

My husband and I have argued about the sky.

He says, *There's no clouds*, with clouds in the background.

He says, *There's no trees*. I say, *I'm looking at a tree right now*. (The squirrel's gravesite.)

You can't just talk about the weather anymore.

There's an urge to tell someone what's happening, but the people who care know, and the people who don't know don't care.

Good luck feels like bad luck waiting to happen, but bad luck still just feels like bad luck.

When good things happen I don't know how to feel.

It's not that I'm conflicted—more that I'm trying to use reason to determine how happy I should be.

At Kennedy Airport I had the experience of wanting to see a famous person and not care. That was a particular experience I wanted to have.

Instead, during that experience, the experience of wanting, I saw someone I know from my own past. Neither of us lives in New York.

Do our experiences belong to us? Are they a property, "like a hat"?

(Wittgenstein says no.)

Do you have to pay attention to your own desires, which you do not own, to be *mindful*?

Can you *not* pay attention to your desires?

Will attention excite or assuage my desire? (You can't observe X without changing X.)

I don't care. I want to change my mind.

The Quality of Nothing (After This Nothing Happened)

"Why is there something rather than nothing?" feels disingenuous, on an ontological level, because we think of even nothing as something.

I think of nothing as empty space in all directions. But emptiness, darkness, is something.

It feels like we'd need some light to see the darkness; we'd need some time to see the space. (Nothing happened before this, because no thing happens in no time.)

It feels like, if space were transparent, we'd have to see something through it on the other side. But nothing has no sides.

The question is, why is there something *or* nothing?

Why that nothing, instead of some other, under-nothing?

Which is more frightening, nothing or empty space?

What's the difference between *scared* and *afraid*?

Is it the difference between a present threat and a future threat? Or a sudden threat and a slow one?

Are there horror stories where the people in the story aren't scared?

Or is all horror fear horror—what's scary is the fear.

If we like scary movies, we must like real horror on some level too.

I like listening to sad music when I'm sad. It doesn't make me feel happier per se, it just improves the quality of the sadness.

More to the point, certain frivolities that used to feel harmless now feel harmful. Choices always feel *personal*.

Personally, I like when decisions feel like they make themselves.

I like to make small decisions that essentially don't matter.

Eye pain feels inherently emotional. The way odd numbers feel more random.

As I get older, I feel less confident, because less self-deceiving.

I sometimes have the feeling that everything in the future is inevitable, yet I have to experience the events as if they weren't.

Or, "the present" is the illusion that we don't know the future.

Samuel Johnson said, "Nothing odd will do long. *Tristram Shandy* did not last." (Not *will* not—*did* not.)

Chief Plenty Coups of the Crow Nation said, "When the buffalo went away the hearts of my people fell to the ground, and they could not lift them up again. After this nothing happened."

After this nothing happened.

Like throwing a paper airplane into a canyon.

Maybe we don't yet understand everything about how this happened.

After the shock comes a feeling that I knew this would happen.

Dramedy

Did you know when unemployment is high
There's a sharp decline in fatal accidents?
Did you know tobacco itself is radioactive?

Who do I think I'm talking to? No one
With a face, with dahlias for eyes,
A train tunnel mouth.

Write the image out.
A new one appears,
Black asterisks on a field of white.

When I'm suffering I don't ask for help.
I'm afraid they'll come and try
To take my pain away.

Concentrate now on the passage of time.
There is no normal rate.
It takes as long as it takes.

I Don't Want to Hear Any Good News or Bad News

The other day I thought of an old enemy and smiled—not with malice, but with fondness. I felt like I missed her.

Happiness and sadness are somehow alike; they both come in waves. Unhappiness is different, just a general malaise.

A Hollywood ending is "an outcome in which all desirable results are achieved." But don't sad movies win more awards?

It's so sad to have once been good at something.

There's a fundamental uselessness to feeling sad about things that happened very far away or in the deep past.

Whatever mechanisms are required to not be sad all the time mean that sometimes when you want to be sad, you can't.

During the Middle Ages, "Poverty, wars, and local famines were so much a part of normal life that they were taken for granted and could therefore be faced in a sober and realistic manner."

Sometimes I involuntarily smile when I hear bad news.

Bad news makes me feel closer to people.

Good news is bad news—sadly bad news is also bad news.

I don't trust the news unless I can't understand it.

News serves a social function more than anything else. Monks don't read the news.

I read in the news that alcohol stimulates the immune system; ants are a liquid.

I read that frogs don't actually just sit in a pot of water until they boil to death. (What kind of sicko would make that up?)

I actually like talking about the weather.

I actually like crying, it makes me feel better.

If all possible worlds don't exist, we might actually live in a very unlikely world. It might not get more unlikely than this.

Supposedly Joe Brainard said on his deathbed: "One good thing about dying. You don't have to go to any more poetry readings."

Bad news: You can't actually save time. You'll just use it to do something else.

You pretty much have to do one thing at a time, and in order.

You could change your life.

You could waste some time and be happy.

I like to feel wistful before sleep, and sometimes I get in bed early just to lie there awake, feeling wistful.

I procrastinate more than I used to, and worry less. It turns out, important stuff just gets done.

I know it will get done. So it seems strange that I actually have to do it.

Why do I have to make this future that already exists?

Historians of the Future

In the late 18th century, people stopped thinking of "Utopia" as a place (a different place at the same time—now) and started thinking of it as a time (the same place—here—at a different time).

Now there are far more dystopias than utopias.

Now we think of both the past and future as dystopias.

Now, a study showed, we have more pop songs in minor keys. Because "people like to think of themselves as smart and complicated."

All my imagined futures have turned into memories.

Today, there's more past than yesterday. But is there any less future?

There's a 10,000-year clock, "The Clock of the Long Now," being built in the mountains of West Texas, from "largely valueless materials."

It's comforting that there's so much more past than present.

There's a period known, in the history of the future, as the eternal now or the ever-present origin. Zero-dimensional.

The eternal now was followed by magic consciousness (one dimension), and then by mythic consciousness, which "knows time but not space" (two dimensions).

Once we know the future, the past is changed.

I don't know all my great-grandparents' names.

My mother can't die until her hair turns gray.

Before we are born, we exist even less than after we die. We should tremble when we think of that time.

How long until we exist so little again?

The past happens fast.

If there was infinite past, the sky would be nothing but starlight. "Observed darkness and nonuniformity of night" make us finite.

There are few stars, moving farther apart.

The past is bright, but black and white. The future is dim but in color.

The past is still. The future trembles.

Yes & No

Driving, alone, at night, with music
Is safe. No visible stars.
A blood orange moon and then Mars.

Lying, in bed, alone, is safe.
Keep your hands clean,
You can touch your own face.

Keep the windows shut. No opening
For spirits: Influenza, evil eye,
Miasma, killer bee. Stray bullet. Flea.

Everything comes back normal.
The image of the aster,
It's all in mental space.

How sublime the moon.
How sublime, the mossy ruins.
The fear and the fear itself.

That It Is Folly to Measure Truth & Error by Our Own Capacity

Distance is a kind of time, which means distance is also a kind of money.

A strange kind of distance. A kind of freedom, maybe.

I kind of feel like I'm brushing up against another layer of the multiverse. Language is fucked. Via some kind of space-time bug.

It's almost hard to call it dystopian because there is a kind of utopia inside the dystopia.

I fear pure subjectivity is a kind of erasure. The people in power will use it against us.

Hate can feel like a kind of power.

I always thought it was weird when people would buy the same kind of dog after their dog died (illusion of continuity) but then we did that with our car?

Isn't it kind of the point of culture to assuage our feeling needless and alone?

I just kind of noticed that my mirror image is twice as far away as the mirror.

I once heard a woman described as "almost very pretty."

Now I remember a shimmer of recognition, like *That's something I might have said.*

Like a capital *E* is kind of a bitchy, pale pink color.

Taupe is grayish brown. Mauve is kind of a dusky pinky purple. *Mauvais* sounds like a color.

Kind of a bright-all-night, false dawn of streetlight on snow.

"Every poem is a description of its own creation . . . a kind of hologram of the mental condition at that moment."

Success is a kind of failure.

Youth is a kind of genius.

Not-suffering is a kind of suffering.

Oral History

I read somewhere that people don't mind a long wait for the elevator as long as there's a mirror in the lobby.

I read that scientists don't know why some girls' ponytails bounce up and down and other girls' swing from side to side.

I read in a blog comment "I feel that hot chicks just like going to public events to be hot" and on some level I kind of agree.

I once read that rich people have to invent new names because the good names get "stolen" by poor people.

I read that the atlas moth is born without a mouth and has one week to mate before it dies of starvation.

I read about a brain-imaging study that showed a dead fish could recognize human emotions.

I read that plants can "hear" themselves being eaten.

I read that Pisces dislike "the past coming back to haunt."

I spend a lot of time waiting around for something wonderful to happen.

I often feel that I'm waiting for an unexpected life-changing force to come from nowhere—but how can it if I expect it?

I feel most myself—most trapped in my self—when I'm bored.

I experience boredom as a kind of luxurious misery.

I read that geologically speaking we are "marooned in time," nothing *interesting* happening for eternity, as far as we're concerned, on either side.

I asked my parents if they think I look like them and they said no.

Genealogy (Such Deep Creases)

I've known all my life that my father's Uncle Joe was killed by his wife.

It was almost a novelty story—a murder in the family!

At twelve or thirteen, I learned she was a serial killer—Joe the third husband she poisoned with arsenic.

He was twenty-six when he died of kidney failure. A handsome, hero pilot, back home safe from the war.

She brought him fresh juice every day in the hospital.

I was in my thirties when I found out Joe's mother—my father's grandmother—my great-grandmother—was "never the same."

Joe was her favorite. Her life was ruined by grief.

This woman, my great-grandmother, her name was Geneva. I had forgotten.

I have a black-and-white photo of Geneva wearing pants, about to ride in a bucket into Carlsbad Caverns.

When our lives overlapped, for five or six years, she seemed already dead, still and silent.

I was forty when I learned there was no suspicion of murder until the wife's young daughter started getting sick too. A life insurance scam.

They exhumed my father's uncle, and Joe's older brother—my father's father—my grandfather—had to identify the body.

We were in a restaurant when my father told me this.

"How long had he been buried?" I said. "Months," he said. "Maybe a year." I thought of the word *decay*.

These people, long dead, became yet more real.

It's taken my whole lifetime to understand they're real.

They say "never forget," but you can't remember things you haven't experienced.

You can't remember things you don't know—but you can remember things you don't know you know.

My best friend gave me a kimono with such deep creases that they never came out in the wash, no matter how many times I washed it.

It makes me think of a study I read about once that said butterflies "remember" being caterpillars.

I wonder what I don't know I remember on the long, boring drive across New Mexico.

It's a good kind of boring—the miles of dead nothing, and then a herd of tiny antelopes.

They make me think of Auden's reindeer, moving *silently and very fast* in their *altogether elsewhere*.

There is the elsewhere in the poem, and the elsewhere of the poem—the deer are double elsewhere.

There is the past of the poem, a postwar poem, and the past in the poem, which is about the fall of Rome, which I never remember.

Maybe now I will remember.

Mirror, Mirror

Are you my golden shadow?
Mon semblable?
Blah blah blah?

We do the same things
Over and over in this life—life
The score of our normal minds.

The man in the fire
Didn't recognize his wife.
Naked, shoeless, her mouth "almost black" . . .

We are like a surfer
On the surface of the sea, who cannot see
The whale underneath. We're there for scale.

The fact refers
But the fact itself isn't anything.
We are far from suffering.

Malice & the Unknown

One night, drunk at a party, William Burroughs
suggested a round of William Tell.

His pretty young wife put a highball glass on her head. It
may have had gin in it.

He shot her in the face, from six feet away.

Burroughs was a good shot—but also very drunk. And
witnesses report he looked shocked by what he'd done.

But William and Joan had never played this game before.

We can never know if he meant to do it. We can never
really know.

We can never, ever, ever, ever know.

This helps me think about infinity.

Increasingly, I do things to distract me from my thoughts.

The distraction helps my thinking.

It complicates my thoughts—it adds a mood, like background music.

It makes me interesting to myself.

I once heard someone say, *That's like drinking to remember*, but I like drinking to remember.

I like when bad things happen, but not the ones I was expecting.

I like when something feels like a placeholder that never got replaced.

I like the feeling of starting to like a thing I used to hate. Like cheating on myself.

I like how you remember your hotel room number for the length of your stay, and then it's gone from your mind forever.

I like to think about infinity, the curve that approaches the asymptote.

I like to think about the difference between hearing someone lie and watching someone lie.

A difference of point of view—their point of view, not mine.

There are orders of infinity, infinite sets that are not only larger but infinitely larger than the first order of infinity—but you know all this.

I like thoughts before they coalesce into "thoughts." Before-thoughts.

I like when people lie a little bit and then admit it.

I like when there are buildings on the sides of mountains.

I like when there's a hole in the roof of a building, to watch clouds blow through.

Norman Mailer, also drunk at a party, stabbed his wife—twice—almost in the heart—but did not kill, did not succeed in killing her.

You know this, you know this.

If there are infinite points between 0 and 1, there is infinite past, infinite points that must stay in the past, where they can be protected.

The past. It's so still.

Bright & Distant Objects

I read a headline that said, "Human hair behind pigeons' lost toes, study finds."

I thought it meant that pigeons were growing human hair . . . behind their toes, their lost toes?

I felt sick with fear.

I read a headline that said, "Just thinking about bright objects changes the size of your pupils."

So how do we know that we're actually experiencing anything?

How do we know that we're not just thinking about objects, bright and distant? Concepts? The future?

What do we know of "the actual"?

If you think about greyhounds, your pulse rate goes down.

I am thinking about 16 Psyche, a metallic asteroid so massive it exerts gravitational disturbances on other asteroids.

Some speculate it's composed of gold and platinum, which would make it worth "quintillion dollars," or billions of times all the money on Earth.

In these terms, everything in the universe is money, a concept humans made up, like emotions.

In the future, objects in the universe will be so far apart that distant civilizations could never discover each other, even theoretically.

They could not even think about each other.

Sometimes, during a period of dread, I momentarily forget the thing I'm dreading, but continue to feel the dread.

Sometimes, I feel like I'm about to remember something, but the memory never arrives—just the all-consuming feeling of *about to*.

Or the memory has arrived, but it's a memory of nothing, with nothing to be about.

The feeling of pure, empty remembering.

If things are just themselves, what do we know of things?

The moon? Clouds? Herons?

Are they decorative objects?

Details on the surface of the actual?

What is a human skull worth—really, what is the cost?

I want to purchase a human skull.

I want to know what happens to desire when you're dead—should your desires be *respected*?

You can have your ashes embedded in a record, so your survivors can listen to your death.

You can turn all the carbon in your body into artificial diamonds—you can want that.

My friend the undertaker wanted to be turned into a diamond, then embedded in his own skull, a decorative object.

An undertaker takes the body under, a coincidence of
language. (It's just a euphemism: *an undertaking*.)

What you wanted, once you're dead, is the real without
feeling.

Desires with no one to want them.

Random Assignment

It seems to want to rain but can't.
It fades to pink, an argument.
Relinquish the dream.

You can't ever get what you want,
You can't please any of the people
Any of the time.

Time just lies there,
Not fast or slow,
Any more than a line.

I wonder if the very small ants are afraid
Of the big ants, if they ever cross paths.
I wonder if happiness is ethical.

I'd like to do it all again
In silence now, in darkness,
A wasp in a fig.

Stop Thinking & End Your Problems

I met a woman with a tumor in her language center. She would think about what she wanted to say, then hear her thought in the voice of the person she was talking to, so it felt like they were reading her mind.

I think there is a name for this, but can't remember what it is.

I think "clarity" is kind of a poorly defined idea.

I think it would still work with more distance.

I think I pray a lot now; prayer just isn't what I thought it was.

Whether or not I believe in God (I don't), "God" is so useful, as language. I can't think without the word *God*.

I think we expect too much of people, who are mostly suffering and confused.

I think we make the mistake of thinking that "history" is truer than experience is true.

I think "grateful to be alive" is a feeling you can maintain for one or two days, tops.

I think every well-meaning critique-of-war film will eventually turn into "explosions look beautiful."

I think if you read a poem, then forget you've read it, and then much later you read it again, it really does get better.

I think maybe sadness and happiness are alike, but unhappiness is different.

I think pleasure is a basic human need, but eating isn't *resistance*, we just need to eat.

If you order hot tea in a restaurant, I automatically think you're not very fun.

Crying must release endorphins or something. I wish I could cry for longer.

I think panic is a decent strategy.

I think of it as a very dramatic form of giving up.

I think it's hard not to experience your life as a thing that happens *to* you.

I think it's fooling yourself into thinking you're thinking.

I do all this mental preparing to the point I think it already happened.

I think it's largely unconscious, feels like a collective decision, not a chain of events.

I think it's philosophical and physical and have not gotten a good answer.

Everything reminds me of it, but I don't know what "it" is.

We Taste Nothing Pure

Saying *outre-mer* really gives one the feeling of looking wistfully out to sea.

It's almost onomatopoeia.

In Korea, someone told me, people go do karaoke in the middle of the day and don't drink or anything. Not even for fun, almost. Just out of habit.

At an art talk, the critic asked the audience who thought of themselves as artists. I almost reflexively raised my hand. He meant *painters*.

There's a culture of anxiety that is almost encouraging: "Go ahead! Feel bad!"

I almost always feel better the day after feeling really bad, but then the next day, I feel a little worse again.

When Robert Lowell read Sylvia Plath's last poems he said they make one feel "almost all other poetry is about nothing."

I finally learned how to read in my dreams—now some dreams are mostly language.

It's almost erotic.

The almost fictive level of detail is disturbing.

I almost applaud the perversity of showing disaster movies on planes.

But planes *aren't* dangerous, compared to almost anything else.

You can only be bored *almost* to death.

I'm almost looking forward to it.

Notoriously, someone dies from alcohol poisoning almost every year.

Almost picked up and drank hot candle wax.

Almost started crying and then got distracted.

It's almost like love depends on a little suffering.

A bottomless, almost Catholic appetite for being scolded.

It's almost like an intentional setup, almost self-sabotage, almost superstitious. It's almost mystical.

It almost feels like you can't say anything interesting about it.

It's not boring to me exactly but it almost feels like something to live through rather than do.

I almost adore it.

I hate it so much sometimes it almost brings me joy.

In Nature

I can think, but rarely of nature.
I look with my back to the landscape,
As if in a Claude glass.

A cheat code. Ninety-nine lives,
Which might as well be infinite
Unless this isn't the first one?

Nietzsche said *There's a rollicking kindness*
That looks like malice.
I ascribe that "kindness" to fate.

A breeze carries unknown pathogens,
Information that can't want to die
Because it's not alive.

What it wants is desire.
A barrier to crossing
The chasm of the day.

The Beginning of Understanding Is the Wish to Die

I've got this one profound thought in me but I don't think you would understand.

I barely understand it myself.

I never understood what was so great about cheekbones.

I still don't understand cairns.

Roko's Basilisk can't ruin your life if you don't understand it.

I want an artist to try to "understand the shape of my mouth."

1. Nobody understands it as well as I do. 2. I don't understand it.

I don't understand why pilots tell you the cruising altitude. Like, what's that got to do with me?

I'm not trying to be rhetorical, I really don't understand.

I didn't understand classic movies at all until I had a martini with vermouth in it.

I don't understand people who say they "love pie."

I'm inclined to think good news is really bad news. It's like I don't trust the news unless I can't understand it.

I read that in physics you have to publish results before you understand them.

I don't understand how people remember what happened this year versus last year versus some other time in the past or future.

Other scientific concepts that "must die": continuity of time, the self, *the* universe.

I understand almost nothing about your life. I don't understand the mentality.

"God is faithful even when I don't understand."

I have high confidence that I will never understand.

Jealousy Is the Gin

Once in my lifetime I heard someone say, *Envy is vermouth, jealousy is gin.*

For years I have pondered, and not understood, what this meant.

Envy is but what we rinse the glass with?

Wanting what others have makes their wanting what you have more delicious?

Vermouth is aged wine, and envy is jealousy plus the dimension of time—

Jealousy is envy remembered, or—

Envy is jealousy pre-remembered, in the future, when we get what we desire.

Envy is not admiration—I want what they have instead of them.

I only envy who I despise.

When I totaled my car, my father advised me to buy a new one outright.

I had the money to do it, but I didn't want to do it.

What I thought was, *Maybe, before the car is paid off . . . I'll die.*

It's like I like the idea of my corpse having debts.

It's like I like the idea of death as a form of general revenge.

I envy the brave—I want someone to be brave—and am glad when they fail.

The failure of others does not interfere with my futurish gaze.

Nietzsche called envy "a slave morality," or *ressentiment*—

Resentment—that is, refeeling.

Your feeling, but now it's mine.

Desiderata

Do you ever get that feeling like something bad just happened but you forgot what it was?

I want to say something negative about it.

I want to say something, but nothing comes to mind that's not a cliché or a lie.

I want someone to apologize to me, but not a specific person, and not for a specific thing.

I want to go to sleep and wake up and not be a terrible person.

I want to donate my personality to science.

I don't *particularly* want to suffer and then die in a war.

I don't want TO DIE, I just want to BE DEAD.

I wish my mind could be freed from this rickety carcass.

I wish "war" didn't have such noble connotations.

I don't understand what's so great about eclipses; we don't want for signs of doom.

I'll go gentle into that good night if I fucking want to.

I want nothing so much as a real operatic cry. Like, on stage.

I wish, at the end of each day, the judges would tell me I'm "safe."

I never close the windows on planes.

People who close the windows on planes: I guess you don't want to feel melancholy and golden and sublime?

I always wanted dramatic, deep-set eyes and a widow's peak.

I want a nightgown to wear as I walk into the sea.

I don't want to feel good, I want to feel sad. Happiness lately feels mostly beside the point.

It's not that I think I deserve punishment. Just weird

fleeting wishes for tragedy. I don't want people to get what they deserve?

What's it called when you want bad things to happen?

Life is usually good/bad/good/bad. So when things are good it's like, Well, this isn't going to last!

When things are bad you can enjoy yourself.

When things are bad do you ever secretly wish for them to get worse?

Like I wanted it to be the same, but more so. I want to feel more of what I'm already feeling.

Maybe it's a subconscious wish.

Part of me never wants it to end.

I wish rich people would stop having beautiful children.

General relativity says that "objects move toward regions where time elapses more slowly; in a sense, all objects 'want' to age as slowly as possible."

Remember when people used to wish for world peace?

I'm making a wish as I throw this nickel in the trash.

I wish men wore ruffs and kilts and cummerbunds. Give me something to look at . . .

I want a house with a tree in it.

I want to wear lipstick in the woods.

I want to relive my life, but not for the first time. Again, from the outside!

I like the idea that someone might think I have impersonators.

I guess I want someone to think I'M the impersonator.

I want to be famous for being obscure. I'm getting closer to this.

I just took a nap and dreamed about it (not kidding).

Just because you fantasize about something doesn't mean you actually want it. People don't know what they want!

Please correct me if I'm wrong, I want to be wrong.

I have a morbid fear of trainers. They always want to help you meet your "goals."

But I don't have goals!

Detail

How is there never a beginning to a dream?

A dream does not begin.

It ends when you wake—but does not begin

When you fall asleep.

Time comes out of time

Like ribbon from cassettes,

Shimmering, sticky,

More than seems possible,

More and more tape

Like time from a dream.

A golden-white silken thread

Of incandescent pain

As thin as nothing,

That immeasurable,

Is pouring like a strand of honey

Into the ocean, out of the

Fog in the mind.

It does not begin.

It goes as high as God.

Awake & Alone

Am I in the wrong history?

I thought in a dream where I watched an instant replay
with a contrary outcome to the one I'd just witnessed.

But the replay in the dream was as real as the dream.

When I'm only alone asleep, I try to reach aloneness
through sleep.

Being alone is first position.

The other day, alone in a room with my friend Mike, he said

What are you doing this weekend?

And after a pause I said

Who, me?

The weird part was, he didn't even think it was weird.

It is so much easier to sit and think in a bar alone than at home.

In a bar where I am not alone

I can remember every thought I've ever thought

And they come back to me, *as* thoughts, as real as the dream.

But now I am awake.

Now that I am finally alone.

The Idea of a Meadow

I've become obsessed with the idea of a meadow, a
meadow I am not in.

Yellow flowers are in the meadow. They must be; they are
part of my idea of a meadow.

There is the yellow on green below, the flowers in the
grass, the white on blue above.

My viewpoint is in the middle, though I'm not in the
meadow.

It forms a white line extending out to the horizon, a line
that is real in the real of the meadow—

When the meadow is real, so is the line.

You can think of the meadow as kind.

But the meadow is indifferent to human life—even to
mine, even my meadow.

My meadow with day moon and trickling stream, rabbit
and magpie.

White wisp of cloud, white snow on the mountain, the
meadow a valley—

There is cloud wisp and flowers, but they are not for me,
when the meadow is real.

I'm not in the meadow. The meadow is not mine.

Don't Think

One way to fall asleep is paradoxical intention: trying not to fall asleep.

So the thinking goes, this reduces your performance anxiety.

The question is, who are you fooling, if you really want to fall asleep?

As if sleep were a performance for God.

The instructions on a sleep mask say, you still need to close your eyes.

I wish the pink light of sunrise lasted longer, the warm pink of in-between.

One way to fall asleep is to say *Don't think* over and over to yourself.

The instructions say, try to practice it mindlessly.

In sleep, sleep becomes an everlasting interlude, an eternal in-between.

I read that staring into space "can help"—but can't remember what it helps with, thinking or not thinking.

Not thinking is the closest we can get to stopping time.

All I know of time is in my mind; my mind is all I know.

Only fifteen minutes ago, I had no idea it was going to snow.

And yesterday, and yesterday, what did we believe?

It's so easy to forget, as if it were a dream.

The future wasn't obvious.

And the old snow on mountains that never would melt—it didn't look real.

Certain Conditions

These are the days of moth and iris.

Under gates and eaves, the moths hang like bats, invisible in shadow.

They all flutter out, hundreds of moths, at the slightest movement.

They are harmless to me, and yet it is difficult not to scream.

A woman tries to run a man over in the street by the Capitol.

She even turns the car around, on a one-way street.

Even without this, I am experiencing a crisis.

I am experiencing a crisis, even without respect to a telic midpoint.

It's become unhelpful to think in terms of years.

But in theory it's pain, not death, I'm afraid of.

My friend recommends I confront my emotions with
RAIN:

Recognize, accept, interrogate, nurture.

She says fear and excitement are somehow the same.

I think of an old military acronym, VUCA: *volatile,
uncertain, complex, and ambiguous.*

It is so redundant as to be extravagant.

My friend's doctor tells her: eight drinks a week is the
limit.

We have a good laugh. Should we live for a future?

Should we live to fight for life, when we hate our own lives?

I think getting what you want is just backwards desire.

And the undoing hurts.

Moon News

I read that in January of 1912, "the moon came closer to the Earth than at any time in the previous 1,400 years."

High tides make the sea extra iceberg-y; ergo, the moon sunk the *Titanic*.

When you turn your concentration to one thing, you turn your distraction to something else. Distraction as dark side of the moon.

Every photo of the moon from the moon looks black and white, because the moon is black and white.

I resent all this news about the moon. I only love the moon when it takes me by surprise.

Here's my favorite thing about the moon: A moonwalker said when he's looking at the sky, he sometimes suddenly remembers: That's *my* moon, the same moon I walked on. (To each their own moon.)

We realize the same things over and over, new every time.

We are born not remembering why we walked into the room.

Notes

The title and last line of "About Suffering" are indebted to Auden's "Musée des Beaux Arts." The phrase "we become lyrical when we suffer" is from a James Longenbach essay (but I didn't remember the source at the time of writing). The line about Turgenev is taken from his biographical note in the Penguin Classics editions of his novels. The phrase "forty minutes of desolate shuffling" is borrowed from Paraic O'Donnell.

In "The Idea of Beginning," the book in question is *A Dictionary of Symbols* by Juan Eduardo Cirlot, translated from the Spanish by Jack Sage and Valerie Miles.

In "I'm Not Mourning," the italicized lines are from Bashō.

The title "That to Philosophize Is to Learn to Die" is from Montaigne. The line in quotes is from *Wikipedia*.

In "I Don't Want to Hear Any Good News or Bad News," the line about the Middle Ages is from *The Pursuit of the Millennium* by Norman Cohn.

In "Historians of the Future," some of the quoted language comes from Jennifer M. Gidley's *The Future: A Very Short Introduction.*

The title "That It Is Folly to Measure Truth & Error by Our Own Capacity" is from Montaigne. The line about a poem as a hologram is from Ted Hughes's *Paris Review* interview.

In "Mirror, Mirror," the phrase "mon semblable" is from "Au Lecteur" by Baudelaire.

"Bright & Distant Objects" is for Janaka Stucky.

"Stop Thinking & End Your Problems" is a line attributed to Lao Tzu.

The title "We Taste Nothing Pure" is from Montaigne.

The title "The Beginning of Understanding Is the Wish to Die" is from Kafka's notebooks. I have lost the source of the "God is faithful" line.

In "Desiderata," the line about general relativity is from *The Hidden Reality* by Brian Greene.

"Certain Conditions" is for Sommer Browning, Erin Costello, and Sarah Rose Etter.

In "Moon News," the first line quotes from a Reddit post that links to an article on the NASA site.

Throughout, there is stray quoted material for which I have lost the original source. Mea culpa.

The fifteen-line poems were all written in the summer of 2020. They are for John Cotter and Michael Joseph Walsh.

Acknowledgments

Some of these poems originally appeared, sometimes in earlier versions, in the following journals and magazines: *American Chordata*, *American Poetry Review*, *The Atlantic*, *Bennington Review*, *The Brooklyn Rail*, *Gulf Coast*, *Iterant*, *The Nation*, *New England Review*, *The New York Review of Books*, *New York Tyrant*, *A Public Space*, *Split Lip*, *Spork*, and *Tupelo Quarterly*. Thank you to the staff and editors, in particular Kaveh Akbar, David Barber, Rick Barot, Anselm Berrigan, Jordan Castro, Marianne Chan, Kristina Marie Darling, Michael Dumanis, Josh English, Brett Fletcher Lauer, Danika LeMay, Jana Prikryl, Sarina Romero, Elizabeth Scanlon, and Bianca Stone. "About Suffering" appeared on the *PoetryNow* podcast; thank you to Michael Slosek, Katie Klocksin, and the Poetry Foundation. "Don't Think" appeared on the *Slowdown* podcast; thank you to Ada Limón.

Thank you to Monika Woods for all your support and guidance. Thank you to Sarah Jean Grimm—I feel lucky you found this book. Thank you to Mensah Demary, Sarah Lyn Rogers, and the gracious staff at Soft Skull. For additional help, various and hard to describe, thank you to Brandon Amico, Sommer Browning, Erin Costello, Todd Dillard, Sarah Rose Etter, Erinrose Mager, Catherine Nichols, Jennifer Olsen, Kathleen Rooney, Selah Saterstrom, Martin Seay, and Michael Joseph Walsh. Thank you to my group chats. Thanks and love to my family. Thanks and love to John Cotter, who told me I should write more poetry.

ELISA GABBERT, a poet, critic, and essayist, is the author most recently of *The Unreality of Memory: And Other Essays* and *The Word Pretty*. She writes a regular poetry column for *The New York Times*, and her work has appeared in *Harper's Magazine*, *The New York Review of Books*, *A Public Space*, and elsewhere. Her next collection of essays, *Any Person Is the Only Self*, is forthcoming from Farrar, Straus and Giroux.